ZONDERKIDZ

The Berenstain Bears'® Bedtime Blessings

Copyright © 2017 by Berenstain Publishing, Inc.
Illustrations © 2017 by Berenstain Publishing, Inc.

This book is also available as a Zondervan ebook.

Requests for information should be addressed to:

Zonderkidz, 3900 *Sparks Dr. SE, Grand Rapids, Michigan* 49546

ISBN 978-0-310-74904-2

All Scripture quotations, unless otherwise indicated, are taken
from The Holy Bible, New International Version®, NIV®. Copyright © 1973, 1978, 1984, 2011 by Biblica, Inc.® Used by permission of
Zondervan. All rights reserved worldwide. www.Zondervan.com. The
"NIV" and "New International Version" are trademarks registered
in the United States Patent and Trademark Office by Biblica, Inc.®

Any Internet addresses (websites, blogs, etc.) and telephone numbers in this
book are offered as a resource. They are not intended in any way to be or
imply an endorsement by Zondervan, nor does Zondervan vouch for the
content of these sites and numbers for the life of this book.

Zonderkidz is a trademark of Zondervan.

Editor: Mary Hassinger
Design: Cindy Davis

Printed in China

17 18 19 20 21 22 23 24 /LPC/ 17 16 15 14 13 12 11 10 9 8 7 6 5 4 3 2 1

By Mike Berenstain
Based on the characters created by
Stan & Jan Berenstain

It was evening in the Bear family's tree house. In fact, it was getting late. The sun had gone down long ago, and the western sky was a deep, glowing blue.

Papa was nodding over his fishing magazine. Mama was trying not to yawn as she worked on a patchwork quilt.

Mama and Papa were growing sleepy, but Brother, Sister, and Honey were still wide-awake. Brother was creating a model of the Mesozoic Age. There were trees and rocks and lots of dinosaurs.

"ROWR! ROWR!" said Brother as he battled a Tyrannosaurus rex against a Triceratops.

DINOS DINOS

Sister was playing with her SuperBear figures. She decided it would be nice if they all had a tea party.

"Would you like another muffin, Mr. Spider Bear?" she asked, politely.

Honey was building a princess castle with blocks. But when it was ready for her princess dolls to move in, she started to feel sleepy. Clearly, she needed something to wake her up.

"Horsey, Papa!" said Honey, hopping onto Papa's lap. "Play horsey!"

"Huh? Wha–?" said Papa, starting out of his doze.

"Horsey! Play horsey!" said Honey.

"Oh!" said Papa, stretching. "Horsey—sure, sweetie-pie. Climb aboard."

Papa boosted Honey onto his back and began galloping around
the room.

"Ride 'em, cowboy!" yelled Brother and Sister.

"Now, Honey. Now, Papa," said Mama. "That certainly looks like fun. But it's time to calm down and get ready for bed."

"Bed!" said the cubs. "It's still early! We're not sleepy yet."

"It is not early," said Mama, pointing to the big grandfather clock.

"Tick, tock—tick, tock," said the clock.

"My, my!" said Papa, checking his watch against the clock. "Eight o'clock, already. You're right, my dear, it's time for bed."

"Aww, Mama! Aww, Papa!" said the cubs.

"That's enough of your 'aww-ing'," said Papa. "Come along—up the stairs with you."

With Honey still on his back, he led the way. The cubs were soon in their pajamas with freshly washed faces and teeth thoroughly brushed.

"Story time! Story time!" said the cubs, pulling the big Storybook Bible down from the shelf. They led Papa to his easy chair and climbed onto his lap.

"What story would you like tonight?" asked Papa, opening the Bible.

"One with lots of battles and fighting!" said Brother. "Like David and Goliath or Samson and the Philistines."

"How about you, Honey?" asked Papa.

"Bunnies and kitties and lots of animals!" she said, thinking of the story of Noah's Ark.

"And you, Sister?" asked Papa.

"Well," said Sister, thoughtfully. "Sometimes I get bad dreams when bedtime stories are too exciting."

Brother and Honey grew thoughtful. Sometimes they had bad dreams too.

"Are there any Bible stories that will give us sweet dreams?" asked Sister.

"Sweet dreams?" said Papa. "There certainly are. I think I know just the one—the story of Jacob's Dream."

He turned the pages and began to read.

"Jacob was the son of Isaac. Abraham, the first Hebrew, was his grandfather.

One time, Jacob went on a journey. Night came and he grew sleepy. But he had no place to stay. So he lay down on the hard ground with a rock for a pillow."

"While Jacob slept, he had a beautiful dream. He dreamed he saw a stairway reaching from the earth to heaven. The angels of God were going up and down the stairway."

"At the top of the stairway, stood God. He said, 'I am the God of your fathers. I will give your children the land where you lie. They will create a great people who will bless the whole world. I will watch over you wherever you go. I will never leave you.'

"When Jacob woke he knew he was in a blessed place and he promised to serve God all his life."

Papa closed the Bible and kissed Brother, Sister, and Honey goodnight. Mama gently lifted a sleepy Honey into her arms.

"Remember," he said, "God and his angels will always watch over you just as they watched over Jacob."

"That *was* a sweet-dreams story," said Sister, snuggling down and thinking of all those angels. "Goodnight, Papa."

"Goodnight, Papa," said Brother.

"Sweet dreams," Papa said. "God bless you!"

And he turned out the light.